The House on
Strange Street

ReadZone Books Limited

www.ReadZoneBooks.com

© in this edition 2016 ReadZone Books Limited

This print edition published in cooperation with Fiction Express, who first published this title in weekly instalments as an interactive e-book.

FICTI●N EXPRESS

Fiction Express
First Floor Office, 2 College Street,
Ludlow, Shropshire SY8 1AN
www.fictionexpress.co.uk

Find out more about Fiction Express on pages 48–49.

Design: Laura Durman & Keith Williams
Cover Image: Bigstock

© in the text 2015 Simon Cheshire
The moral right of the author has been asserted.

ISBN 978-1-78322-580-4

Printed in Malta by Melita Press.

The House on Strange Street

Simon Cheshire

What do other readers think?

Here are some comments left on the Fiction Express blog
about this book:

"I really like your books. I can't wait for your next chapter."
Iqra, Telford

*"This book is really nice. I really enjoyed it and can't
wait for the next one."*
Eman, Bradford

"This book sounds interesting!"
Gursharon, Southall

Contents

Chapter 1

House for Sale

"That's the strangest house I've ever seen," said Joel.

"It looks scary, too," said his sister Zoe.

"Hmm," said their dad. "It's not very cosy, is it?"

Dad, Joel and Zoe were standing outside the house. They looked up at it. They looked at the other houses in Strange Street. They all looked normal, except this one. It was an odd shape. It was very old and scruffy. Some tiles had fallen off the roof. The windows were broken and chipped.

In the small, tangled front garden was a crooked wooden sign on a post. It said "For Sale".

"We're not really going to live here, are we?" said Zoe.

"We might have to," said Dad. "It's much cheaper than the other houses we've looked at."

"It's horrible," said Joel. He pulled a face.

A big white car drew up. A man in a smart suit got out. He smoothed his hair and beamed a smile at them. He shook Dad's hand.

"I'm Mr Dripp," he said. "I'm selling this beautiful house."

They all looked back at the house. It didn't look *that* beautiful at all.

"As you can see," said Mr Dripp, "it's a lovely family home."

Joel raised his eyebrows at Zoe. She giggled.

Mr Dripp took a jangling set of keys from his pocket. "I'll show you around," he said.

The rusty, ancient key turned in the lock with a loud KA-KLUNG. The house suddenly seemed to shudder. It was as if something inside had just woken up.

"Of course, it does need a little work on it," said Mr Dripp. "But it will look wonderful… one day!"

He swung the front door open. It made a long, eerie CREEEEEEAK.

An icy chill rippled out of the house. All four of them shivered.

"The heating system might need fixing," said Mr Dripp.

Chapter 2

Funny Noises

Dad, Joel and Zoe entered a large, dark and dusty hallway. The door thudded shut behind them. Joel and Zoe thought they heard a low, moaning sound. It came from upstairs.

"What was that?" whispered Joel.

"Probably nothing," his sister whispered back.

"Oh, don't worry about that," said Mr Dripp cheerfully. "Old houses can make funny noises."

A damp, musty smell was clinging to their noses. The air in the hall was thick and clammy.

"It, umm, needs some windows opening," said Dad, sniffing.

"Lots of space in this hall," said Mr Dripp hurriedly, "lovely family home!"

"Are those mushrooms growing on the wall?" Zoe asked.

"I can't tell," said Joel, "the cobwebs are blocking my view."

Dad started asking Mr Dripp about the local area. While they talked, Joel and Zoe wandered slowly across the hall. They peered around, fearfully. The floorboards squeaked beneath their feet. Through a wide arch, they could see a dark, empty living room.

Suddenly, a shadow slid past them! It vanished into the gloom ahead.

"What was that?" whispered Joel. "Something moved!"

"Yes," said Zoe, "just for a... No, we mustn't be silly! This house is old and dirty. But that doesn't mean it's full of monsters or something! It was just a trick of the light. Come on."

She walked into the living room. Joel followed.

At that moment…

Chapter 3

Spookier and Spookier

Joel stopped.

"What was that?" he said.

"What?" said Zoe.

"I heard a voice," Joel replied. "It whispered something."

"Just the wind," said Zoe.

They both listened. For a full minute, they heard no sound. Then... a soft voice spoke, but they could not hear the words.

"It must be Dad and Mr Dripp," said Zoe.

"No," said Joel. "They're behind us. The voice is coming from in front of us. Listen!"

They listened. The voice got closer.

"Beware," it hissed. "Beware the ghosts of Strange Street."

Joel and Zoe clutched each other in terror.

"Let's get out of here!" cried Joel.

They turned. The arch they'd just walked under had gone!

* * *

Meanwhile, in the hall, Dad and Mr Dripp were still talking about the house.

"These stairs look rotten," said Dad.

"Oh," said Mr Dripp quickly, "just a touch of paint, and they'll be good as new! Lovely family home."

"I want to see the bedrooms," said Dad, treading carefully on the first step.

Neither of them had noticed that there was now a solid wall where the arch had been.

Chapter 4

The Door that Wasn't There

In the living room, Joel and Zoe were getting more and more scared.

"Let's yell for help!" cried Joel.

They yelled for help. Dad and Mr Dripp couldn't hear them through the wall.

"Let's get out through the window!" cried Joel.

It was blocked by a mass of tall

stinging nettles, growing outside.

The spooky voice spoke again. Now it seemed to come from everywhere at once. "Beware, the ghosts of Strange Street. We do not like to be disturbed."

"We'll have to go through that door," said Zoe.

"What door?" said Joel.

"That one there," said Zoe. "On the other side of the room."

"That wasn't there before either," said Joel.

"Wasn't it?" said Zoe. "Perhaps we just didn't see it. Maybe it was hidden in the shadows?" She took a step towards the door.

"Be careful. It could be a trap," said Joel.

"We'll have to risk it," said Zoe. "That door is now the only way out. Come on."

Joel and Zoe crept forward. They inched closer to the door.

Suddenly, the door handle began to turn slowly. The door creaked open all on its own. They stepped through and peered into the gloom.

"Poo!" cried Joel. "What's that smell?"

"It's like last week's school dinner," said Zoe, holding her nose.

"I can't see a thing," whispered Joel. "Anything could be in here with us!"

Luckily, Zoe had a torch on her keyring. She switched it on.

In the glow from the torch, they were amazed at where they found themselves….

Chapter 5

Into the Darkness

In the torchlight, they could see rocks of many strange colours. They could see patches of slippery green and orange slime. The sound of dripping water came from the darkness.

"We're in a cave," said Zoe. Her voice echoed.

"A cave?" cried Joel. "In the middle of a house? This is getting too strange. I don't like it. Let's go back."

They turned. The door had gone!

"I think all these spooky things are happening for a reason," whispered Zoe.

"You think someone is leading us this way?" asked Joel.

"Yes," replied Zoe. "First, the arch vanished, remember? Now the door has disappeared. Someone wanted us to end up in this cave."

"Why are we whispering?" said Joel.

"Shh!" whispered Zoe. "Whoever

led us this way might be hiding somewhere. In the dark."

Zoe swung the torch slowly. Slimy rock… more slimy rock… and then….

Chapter 6

Ghostly Figures

Something rushed at them out of the darkness! There was a loud squeaking sound.

"Mice?" cried Zoe.

"Bats!" cried Joel.

They both screamed with fright. They flapped their arms about. Zoe dropped the torch. The light went out. They screamed with fright again.

The bats flew around their heads, squeaking. At last, they disappeared. Joel and Zoe were left in the dark. Now the only sounds were their own hearts pounding.

"I don't like this," whispered Joel. "Find the torch, can't you?"

Zoe felt about on the floor. "Not without a light to see it, no," she grumbled.

Their eyes got used to the darkness. They saw two faint shapes, glowing in the distance. The shapes were getting nearer… and nearer.

Joel and Zoe hid behind a big rock. They peeped over it.

Two very pale figures floated by. Then they stopped. They glowed in the darkness. One was a girl, one was a boy. They were about Joel and Zoe's age. They were dressed in clothes like Joel and Zoe had seen in history books.

"Where did they go?" said the boy in a ghostly voice. "Their lantern went out."

"I can't see them." said the girl.

"All will be well, as long as they're in the cave," said the boy. "I've set another trap. They'll fall through a hole in the ground. They'll find themselves in our old bedroom."

"Why will that frighten them?" asked the girl.

"Because I filled it with spiders and slugs!" The boy replied.

"Hee hee," chuckled the girl. "That should do it. Now they'll *never* want to live in Strange Street."

"Let's sneak out," said the boy. "Only we know the safe way. Those two will soon fall into the next trap."

"We can set up some scares for the two grown-ups," said the girl.

They floated away. Joel and Zoe stayed hidden in the darkness.

"They're trying to frighten us away," hissed Zoe.

"Why?" whispered Joel. "Who are they?"

"Let's follow them," Zoe replied. "So we won't fall into their trap."

Chapter 7

A Monstrous Trick

The two ghosts floated deep into the cave. Joel and Zoe tiptoed after them. They had to step carefully. The only light was the faint glow of the ghosts.

"We mustn't lose them," whispered Zoe, "or we won't be able to see a thing!"

The ghosts arrived at a window.

It was set into the rock wall of the cave.

"This house gets stranger and stranger," whispered Joel.

The ghosts quietly slid the window open and dived through. They giggled. The window began to slide shut again.

"After them!" said Zoe.

Quick as a flash, Joel and Zoe threw themselves through the closing gap.

Suddenly, they found themselves falling down, down, down. Then up, up, up! Then sideways!

"Whoooaaaaa!" cried Zoe.

"Arrrgghhhh!" cried Joel.

They landed with a bump in another room. There were greasy tiles on the walls. A rusty old metal bathtub stood on the floor. Its tap drip, drip, dripped. There was no sign of the ghosts.

"We're upstairs," said Joel. "In the bathroom. How did *that* happen?"

"And we've lost those ghosts," said Zoe.

"At least we're safe," said Joel. He tried the door.

"Safe but locked in," said Zoe.

A strange gurgling sound echoed around the room. It got louder.

Suddenly a roaring sound came out of the toilet. A deep voice boomed out. "I am the snake-monster of Strange Street. Go away. Leave this house. You're not wanted here." Joel and Zoe looked at each other in alarm.

Chapter 8

A Discovery

"Ghosts, disappearing doors, caves, monsters. I've had enough of this," said Joel, rattling the door handle hard.

"Wait," Zoe said. "I'm sure I know that voice."

"So do I," replied Joel. "It's the snake-monster of Strange Street."

"No it isn't," said Zoe, clicking her

fingers. "It's that boy ghost. The one we saw in the cave."

"No it isn't," growled the monster. But his voice didn't sound quite so 'monstery' now.

"Who are you?" Joel demanded.

"And why are you trying to scare us away?" Zoe asked.

"That's for you to find out." The ghost-monster replied. The gurgling noise returned. Then it went quiet.

"Right, let's get out of here," said Zoe. She strode over to the bathroom door. Taking hold of the handle, she pulled with all her might. The door opened instantly, sending Zoe tumbling to the floor. "Ouch!"

They heard a girl giggling outside.

Zoe leapt to her feet and dashed into the hallway. "I can hear you laughing," she shouted. "I know you're there!" But the ghost girl was nowhere to be seen.

"Maybe we should go and find Dad," Joel said. "We can tell him we don't want to live in this house."

"I don't know," said Zoe. "I don't think the ghosts mean us any real harm. They're just being naughty and playing tricks. We could try to make friends with them. Perhaps it would be fun to live in a haunted house. We could scare all our friends."

Chapter 9

The Mystery Solved

Zoe thought carefully. "We need to talk to those ghosts," she said. "And I know just how to find them!"

She began to speak in a loud voice. "Oh! I am SO scared! Oh! This house is sooooo scary!"

She waved a hand at Joel, to make him do the same.

Joel frowned. He didn't understand

what she was up to. "Umm," he said loudly, "OK. Oh, I'm really scared! I'm so scared… er… I'm going to scream."

They heard giggles coming from nearby.

"They'll run away soon," the boy ghost whispered.

"One more big scare should do it," the girl ghost replied.

"It's working," said Zoe to Joel. "They think they're scaring us. Now they'll come out where we can see them."

"Right," said Joel, nodding his head.

"When they do," Zoe went on, "act as if nothing's happening."

Suddenly, the ghosts shot out of a bedroom! They had become giant-sized! They had put on scary masks! They waved their arms and made scary noises!

Zoe and Joel acted as if nothing strange was happening.

"Oh, hello," said Zoe. "I'm Zoe and this is Joel."

"Hi," Joel grinned.

The ghosts shrunk to normal size. They took off their masks. They looked disappointed.

"We thought you were scared," moaned the boy ghost.

"Oh no," groaned the girl ghost. "Our plan hasn't worked."

"No, it hasn't," said Joel. "And we want to know why you are trying to scare us away."

Chapter 10

A Lovely Family Home

The ghosts looked at each other. They were puzzled. "People don't usually like living in a haunted house," the girl ghost explained. "They always try to send ghosts like us away. This is our home – we don't want to leave." She sighed heavily.

"Well, we don't want you to go anywhere," said Zoe. "We were hoping we could all be friends."

"We've lived on our own here for over a hundred years," said the girl ghost. "I suppose it would be nice to have someone else to play with."

"That's true," agreed the boy ghost. "I'm Rufus and this is Mary."

"This is going to be fun," Zoe grinned. "Who wants to have a normal house when you can live in a haunted one?"

They all laughed.

"We'd better not tell our Dad about you, though," said Joel. "He'd freak out."

"Grown-ups are so silly," said Zoe, rolling her eyes.

"Right," nodded Rufus and Mary.

Zoe had a sudden thought. "Quick! We need to make sure Dad says 'yes' to this house!" She dashed down the stairs.

"You two stay hidden here," Joel said to the ghosts. Then he followed after Zoe.

They ran down into the hall. Dad and Mr Dripp were still talking.

"Just a dab of paint here and there and it will be as good as new," said Mr Dripp. "It's a lovely family home."

Zoe and Joel ran up to Dad.

"We want to live here!"

"This is the house for us!"

"Really?" asked Dad, surprised. "I was about to turn it down."

Mr Dripp went very pale.

"No, it's perfect!" cried Joel.

"Please can we live here, Dad, please," Zoe begged.

"OK, then," laughed Dad. "I suppose we'll take it."

"Hooray, whoopee!" cheered Zoe and Joel. They were sure they could hear the ghosts joining in upstairs.

Mr Dripp grinned from ear to ear.

The four of them headed for the front door. Mr Dripp opened it for them. The door creaked loudly.

"There's a lot of work to be done," said Dad. "This creaky front door needs a bit of oil, for a start."

As they left the house, Joel and Zoe turned.

Rufus and Mary were peering out of one of the bedroom windows. They waved to their new friends. Joel and Zoe waved back.

"It's going to be fun living on Strange Street," said Joel.

"And in such a lovely family home," grinned Zoe.

THE END

FICTI●N EXPRESS

THE READERS TAKE CONTROL!

Have you ever wanted to change the course of a plot, change a character's destiny, tell an author what to write next?

Well, now you can!

'The House on Strange Street' was originally written for the award-winning interactive e-book website Fiction Express.

Fiction Express e-books are published in gripping weekly episodes. At the end of each episode, readers are given voting options to decide where the plot goes next. They vote online and the winning vote is then conveyed to the author who writes the next episode, in real time, according to the readers' most popular choice.

www.fictionexpress.co.uk

WINNER
Education Resources
Award for Innovation

FICTI●N EXPRESS

TALK TO THE AUTHORS

The Fiction Express website features a blog where readers can interact with the authors while they are writing. An exciting and unique opportunity!

FANTASTIC TEACHER RESOURCES

Each weekly Fiction Express episode comes with a PDF of teacher resources packed with ideas to extend the text.

"The teaching resources are fab and easily fill a whole week of literacy lessons!"
Rachel Humphries, teacher at Westacre Middle School

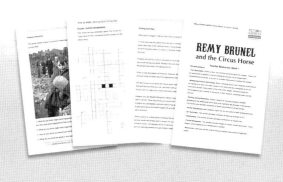

FICTI●N EXPRESS

Deena's Dreadful Day
by Simon Cheshire

Deena is preparing for her big moment – a part in the local talent contest – but everything is going wrong. Her mum and dad are no help, and only her dog, Bert, seems to understand.

Will Deena and Bert make it to the theatre in time? Will her magic tricks work or will her dreadful day end in disaster?

ISBN 978-1-78322-569-9

Emery the Explorer: A Jungle Adventure
by Louise John

When the postman delivers half of a mysterious treasure map through Emery's letterbox, the young explorer knows that a new adventure is about to begin. The trail leads him and his pet monkey, Spider, deep into the steamy Amazon jungle.

Can Emery survive the dangers of the rain forest? Will he succeed in finding the treasure before Dex D Saster, his biggest rival, or will his jungle adventure end in failure?

ISBN 978-1-78322-570-5

FICTI●N EXPRESS

The Sand Witch
by Tommy Donbavand

When twins Chris and Ella are left to look after their younger brother on a deserted beach, they expect everything to be normal, boring in fact. But then something extraordinary happens! Will the Sand Witch succeed in passing on her sandy curse in this exciting adventure?

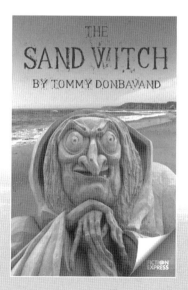

ISBN 978-1-78322-544-6

The Rise of the Rabbits
by Barry Hutchison

When twins Harvey and Lola are given the school rabbit, Mr Lugs, to look after for the weekend, they're both very excited. That is until the rabbit begins to mutate and decides the time has come for bunnies to rise up and seize control.

It's up to Harvey and Lola to find a way to return Mr Lugs and his friends to normal, before the menaces sweep across the country – and then the world!

ISBN 978-1-78322-540-8

FICTI●N EXPRESS

Snaffles the Cat Burglar
by Cavan Scott

When notorious feline felon Snaffles and his dim canine sidekick Bonehead are caught red-pawed trying to steal the Sensational Salmon of Sumatra, not everything is what it seems. Their capture leads them on a top-secret mission for the Ministry of Secret Shenanigans.

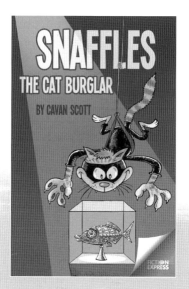

ISBN 978-1-78322-543-9

FICTI●N EXPRESS

The Vampire Quest
by Simon Cheshire

James is an ordinary boy, but his best friend Vince is a bit...
odd. For one thing, it turns out that Vince is a vampire. His
parents are vampires, too. And so are the people who live
at No. 38. There are vampires all over the place, it seems,
but there's nothing to worry about. They like humans, and
they'd never, ever do anything...horrible to them. Unless...
the world runs out of Feed-N-Gulp, the magical vegetarian
vampire brew. Which is exactly what's just happened....

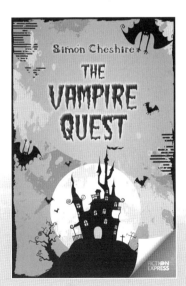

ISBN 978-1-78322-553-8

Simon Cheshire

Simon Cheshire is an award-winning children's writer who has been visiting schools, libraries and literary festivals for well over a decade. He's done promotional book tours around various parts of the UK and America, he's written and presented a number of radio programmes, but he has yet to achieve his ambition of going to the Moon.

Simon was a dedicated reader from a very young age, and started writing stories when he was in his teens. After he turned thirty and finally accepted he'd always have the mind of a ten-year-old, he began creating children's stories and at last found his natural habitat. Since his first book appeared in 1997, his work has been published in various countries and languages around the world.

He's written for a broad range of ages, but the majority of his work is what he calls "action-packed comedies" for 8-12 year olds. He lives in Warwick with his wife and children, but spends most of his time in a world of his own.